Hocus-pocus

Look for more

titles:

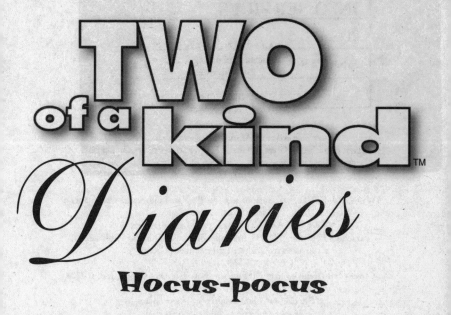

TWO of a kind™ Diaries

Hocus-pocus

by Louise A. Gikow

from the series created by Robert Griffard
& Howard Adler

HarperCollins*Entertainment*
An Imprint of HarperCollins*Publishers*

A PARACHUTE PRESS BOOK

A PARACHUTE PRESS BOOK

Parachute Publishing, L.L.C.
156 Fifth Avenue
Suite 325
NEW YORK
NY 10010

First published in the USA by Harper*Entertainment* 2004
First published in Great Britain by HarperCollins*Entertainment* 2005
HarperCollins*Entertainment* is an imprint of HarperCollins*Publishers* Ltd,
77 - 85 Fulham Palace Road, Hammersmith, London W6 8JB

TWO OF A KIND characters, names and all related indicia are trademarks of
Warner Bros.™ & © 2000.
TWO OF A KIND books created and produced by
Parachute Publishing, L.C.C. in cooperation with Dualstar Publications,
a division of Dualstar Entertainment Group, Inc.

Cover photograph courtesy of Dualstar Entertainment Group, Inc. © 2004

The HarperCollins children's website address is
www.harpercollinschildrensbooks.co.uk

1 3 5 7 9 10 8 6 4 2

ISBN 0 00 718093 4

Printed and bound in Great Britain by Clays Ltd, St Ives plc

Chapter 1

Wednesday

Dear Diary,

Boo!

Hah! Did I scare you, Diary? Sorry – I just couldn't help myself. It's that time of year again! Halloween is less than two weeks away.

I know I'm supposed to be past all that trick-or-treating stuff. But I still think Halloween is cool.

I like carving pumpkins and decorating our room. (Everyone in the First Form – that's seventh grade – at my boarding school, the White Oak Academy for Girls, decorates her room for Halloween.)

I like seeing all the little kids in their costumes. They are really cute.

And, of course, I love, love, *love* Halloween candy.

I even like the color orange. As a matter of fact, my favorite local sports team – the Hampshire Hoops – have orange and white jerseys.

Let's see . . . what other orange things do I like?

Scree scree screeeeee . . .

The scratching sound startled me out of my orange thoughts. "What's that?" I asked.

My roommate, Campbell Smith, looked up from her textbook. She ran her fingers through her short brown hair. It stuck out in jagged spikes around her face.

I didn't bother to tell her about her hair. Campbell doesn't worry about how it looks, except on special occasions. Studying in our dorm room is not a special occasion! At the moment, she was wearing an oversized Boston Red Sox T-shirt (she has about ten of them) and a pair of baggy sweatpants. Campbell is a big Red Sox fan. She's totally into sports, and is the pitcher on our school baseball team, the Mighty Oaks.

"I think there's something scratching on the window," she said, narrowing her brown eyes.

Scree scree screeeeee . . .

I stared at the window between our beds. What could be making that noise?

"Well," I said, a little nervously. "We live on the second floor of Porter House. It's probably a tree branch or something banging against the window."

Campbell frowned. "I don't think it's a tree branch," she said. "There's something weird about it. . . . It's scratching in a kind of pattern."

Scree scree screeeeee . . .

I listened hard. Campbell was right. The scratching was very regular. A little chill went down my back.

Hocus-pocus

"Should we go look to see what it is?" Campbell asked me.

"I-I guess so," I said.

We both stood up from our desks and stared out the window. All we could see was blackness. Neither one of us moved.

I shook off my inner squeamies. "Come on, Campbell," I declared. "There's no reason to be scared. I'm sure it's nothing."

We both slowly walked to the window. The night sky was pitch black. For a minute, I couldn't see anything.

Scree scree screeeeeee!

Suddenly a ghostly white face peered in at us through the glass! It had a leering smile, pointy teeth, and red eyes.

Campbell shrieked and grabbed my arm.

I just stood there. I didn't say a word.

Was I speechless? Petrified with fear? Did I scream?

No way, Diary. I laughed.

"It's just my cousin, Jeremy," I told Campbell, rolling my eyes. "He's trying to scare me . . . again."

Jeremy Burke goes to the nearby Harrington Academy for Boys. He's twelve – the same age as my sister Ashley and me.

"Jeremy has been trying to scare us on Halloween ever since Ashley and I were five years old," I told Campbell.

The creepy face outside moved slowly back and forth. "Whooooooooooo," Jeremy moaned.

"That first year," I said, ignoring Jeremy's groans, "he got dressed up in one of his mom's white sheets and pretended to be a ghost.

"One problem, though," I continued, "it was a queen-sized sheet. Jeremy got all tangled up in it and fell down the stairs."

"Did he get hurt?" Campbell asked, gazing out the window at Jeremy in the mask.

"Actually, he was lucky," I said. "There was so much sheet wrapped around him that he didn't hurt himself at all. But," I added, giggling, "he *did* get in a lot of trouble. He had cut holes in the sheet for his eyes, nose, and mouth. Since it was one of his mom's best sheets, she yelled at him for a whole hour!"

"Whoooo-ooooo!" Jeremy groaned louder and louder. "Whoooo-oooooooooooooo!" He tapped on the window.

"He's been trying to scare us every year since," I told Campbell. "He's put on skeleton costumes, goblin costumes, vampire costumes, ghoul costumes, and one very ugly E.T. costume."

4

Hocus-pocus

Campbell studied the mask still staring at us through the window. "I guess he's pretending to be the Shroud in the movie *The Ghost of Cragun County*."

I shrugged. "No matter what costume he puts on, Jeremy is just not a good scarer. He can't even get to Ashley – and you know what a scaredy-cat *she* is."

Diary, Ashley is the kind of person who doesn't ever go to horror movies. Me? I love them.

That's one of the ways my sister Ashley and I are totally different – even though everybody thinks we look alike. We do both have long, wavy strawberry-blonde hair and blue eyes, and we're the same size. In fact, we could trade clothes – if we didn't have totally different taste. I go for sporty and casual. She's into more trendy and fashionable stuff.

But one thing we both agree on: Jeremy will never, ever be able to frighten us.

Campbell's eyes were still glued to the window. "What is he doing out there?" she asked.

"Whooooo-whooooo!" Jeremy shouted. The mask moved from side to side. "Whooo-whooo! Whoo – whoa! *Whoa!*"

Jeremy's groans suddenly changed to yelps. His arms spiraled wildly. "Whoa!"

There was a big cracking sound. The branch he was sitting on broke.

Campbell and I raced to the window. For the first time ever, Jeremy actually managed to scare me! Was he okay?

I flung open the window and peered out.

I spotted Jeremy clinging to a vine below the window. "Phew," I said. He didn't seem hurt.

"Do you think he's okay?" Campbell cried.

"Probably," I said, hurrying toward the door. "Jeremy somehow always bounces back. But we should go down to check."

Sure enough, when we got there, Jeremy was on his feet, brushing some leaves off his black sweater. He seemed totally fine.

So fine, he still kept up his Halloween act.

"Whoo," he said when he saw us. He raised his arms over his head and waved them weirdly. "Whoo whoo."

Campbell and I just giggled.

"Whoo to you, too," I said. "Are you okay?"

"Yeah, I guess," he grumbled. "So you knew who I was, huh?"

"Yeah," I said, grinning.

"Nice mask," Campbell said.

"Thanks." Jeremy took it off, revealing his blonde curls and grey eyes. I'd almost think he was cute – if he weren't such a pain.

Hocus-pocus

"It didn't work, did it?" He held up the mask.

Campbell shook her head. "Nope."

"Jeremy, look," I told him. "Why don't you just give up? I don't believe in ghosts, ESP, extraterrestrials – none of that stuff. Which makes me almost impossible to scare."

"Just wait," Jeremy taunted. "This was only the beginning. This year, I've got a foolproof plan. And when I'm through, you and Ashley will know the meaning of the word 'fear.'"

"Oh, puh-lease, Jeremy," I said. "You're never going to scare me . . . not ever."

Jeremy's eyes narrowed.

"That's what you think," he said. Then he turned and walked down the path toward the Harrington school.

"Jeremy is hopeless," Campbell said.

"I know," I agreed.

But I couldn't help wondering.

Jeremy sounded awfully sure of himself.

What was his big plan to scare me and my sister?

Dear Diary,

Do you want to hear something truly awesome?

I thought of the absolute best idea

for my article in the next edition of *The White Oak Acorn*, the White Oak Academy school paper!

Here's what happened.

Earlier today, my roommate, Phoebe Cahill, and I went to an editorial meeting for *The Acorn*. I was surprised to see Jill Jenkins there. She's a new First Former and had never come to a meeting before.

I like Jill. She's very quiet, but she's really nice. She showed up at school a few weeks ago. Her folks move around a lot or something, so she couldn't get here at the start of the term. Maybe that's why she seems a little shy.

But she's no pushover, Diary. I'll give you an example. Turns out, the reason she came to the meeting was because Ms. Bloomberg suggested she take photographs for *The Acorn*.

Ms. Bloomberg is our faculty adviser on the paper. She had seen some of Jill's pictures, and she was impressed. She passed around Jill's photographs during the meeting.

Jill didn't say a word. In fact, she seemed embarrassed to be getting all the attention. She sat back in her seat and kept her eyes down, as if she wanted to disappear.

I really liked the pictures. So did Phoebe – she

writes for *The Acorn*, too. In fact, everybody liked the pictures – except for Dana Woletsky.

You probably know, Diary, that Dana isn't my favorite person. She's been pretty obnoxious to me and my sister, Mary-Kate. She really thinks she's the queen of the world. Unfortunately, she's the editor of *The Acorn*, so she was at the meeting, too.

Jill's photos were in black and white. She had portraits of all types of older people – some looked ancient and wrinkly, some looked wise and calm, a few had exotic features and clothing. She also had photos of landscapes that seemed sort of lonely and a little strange.

"Pretty cool, huh?" Phoebe whispered to me.

"Yeah," I whispered back. "I like them."

But Dana didn't. And she was really snotty about it. "You know," she said, looking Jill up and down, "we're a school newspaper. This stuff is kind of" – Dana pointed at a picture of a white-haired lady in a shawl – "fake and dramatic, don't you think?"

For the first time, Jill sat forward in her chair. "That's a picture of my grandmother," she said. "And believe me . . . she's not fake at all."

Dana blinked. Of course she had nothing to say after that. Even Dana knows when she's put her foot in her mouth.

Although she's artistic, Jill isn't into fashion at all. She dresses really simply, in preppy pleated skirts and plain white T-shirts, mostly. It's practically her uniform. She says she doesn't really care how she looks – just how other people look through her camera lens.

But I've got to admit I can't wait to get to know her better, so I can do one of my makeovers on her. A little jewellery, some lip gloss, and the right clothes, and she could be soooo cute. . . .

Anyway, back to my story. After the meeting, Phoebe and I invited Jill to join us for frozen decaf mochaccinos in town. I was really glad when she said yes.

"I hope a mochaccino will help me come up with a brilliant concept for the paper for tomorrow's meeting," I said as we walked to Lots o' Latte.

"I don't want to do just another feature on Halloween." Phoebe shook her head, making her brown curls bounce a little. "*The Acorn* does that every year.

"What do you think about a piece on some great poets – like Robert Frost?" she went on. "I could talk about how he wrote about the seasons. Like that poem, 'Stopping by Woods on a Snowy Evening.'" Phoebe's vintage-print skirt swirled

around her ankles as she walked. "'Whose woods
these are I think I know . . .'" she quoted, flinging
out her arms dramatically.

Phoebe's eyes were shining behind her blue-
framed glasses. She really loves poetry.

"I don't know," I said. "Like Dana said, *The Acorn*
is a newspaper. Poetry would fit better in a literary
magazine. We need to write about stuff that's
happening at school."

"What are you writing about, Ashley?" Phoebe
asked.

I shook my head. "I'm not sure," I admitted. "I
was thinking of doing something on fall fashions –
what White Oak kids are wearing this year." I
glanced at Jill. "What about you, Jill? Do you have
any ideas?"

"Well, I thought I could take pictures of the
trees," Jill said. "I usually just photograph in black
and white, but the colors here in New Hampshire
are so great. It's completely different from the place
I lived before."

"Where was that?" I asked.

"Oh, just around," Jill said. She twirled a strand
of her long, light brown hair around her finger.

"Your idea is really good," Phoebe told her. "It is
gorgeous around here. And maybe I could sneak in

some poetry, too. I could find autumn poems to go along with Jill's photographs."

As we approached the front of Lots o' Latte I noticed the large, brightly coloured poster in the window. It showed some acrobats and a few clowns posed in a circus ring. "Look," I said, pointing to the poster. "The Stars Circus and Carnival. I wonder when it's coming to town."

We all crowded around the poster to check it out. "October twenty-first. Wow! That's tomorrow!" Phoebe said.

My eyes lit up. "I can't wait to go!"

And, Diary, that's when I had my brainstorm.

"Hey!" I exclaimed. "Why don't I write a piece for *The Acorn* about the circus? I could interview all the performers and find out what being in a circus is really like. And Jill – you could take the pictures."

"That's a great idea!" Phoebe said. "Maybe I could do a sidebar article to go along with yours. A history of circuses around the world."

"That would be awesome!" I turned to Jill. So far she hadn't said a word. "Don't you think so, Jill?"

"I don't know," Jill said, frowning. "I mean . . . the circus. Isn't it sort of . . . babyish? Who's going to want to read about a circus?"

Hocus-pocus

"Everybody!" I declared. "The circus has acrobats and clowns. . . . It can be a real behind-the-scenes investigation."

Jill shook her head. "I'm not so sure it's a good idea," she said slowly.

"How come?" Phoebe asked her.

Jill shrugged. "I just don't think First Formers will be interested," she said. "I mean, can you imagine Dana Woletsky having fun at the circus?"

I laughed. "You have a point there," I said. "But Dana doesn't get to tell us what we can write."

"I think the other kids will be really interested," Phoebe said. "Circuses have been around forever. And there's a kind of magic to them."

"Sounds like the beginning of your article," I said, smiling.

I turned to Jill. "Think about it," I told her. "The pictures you can take will be amazing! There are all the people who work at the fair, and behind the scenes at the circus. Imagine taking pictures of the acrobats as they swing from their flying trapezes – "

"And the clowns!" Phoebe chimed in. "Talk about colourful!"

"Clowns?" Jill looked at us. "Why would anyone at White Oak Academy be interested in a bunch of clowns?"

We argued about it the whole time while we ordered our frozen drinks and then during our walk back to school. But we couldn't get Jill excited about the idea. In fact, the more we talked, the more stubborn she got.

"I don't understand," I told Phoebe when we were back in our room. "I don't know Jill very well, but she seemed to really want to be a part of *The Acorn*."

"I know," Phoebe said. She looked as confused as I felt.

"Why is she so against the idea of doing an article about the circus?" I asked.

Phoebe just shook her head and shrugged.

Well, Diary, I've made a decision. I'm going to present my idea at tomorrow's editorial meeting – no matter what. If Jill won't take the pictures, then Ms. Bloomberg will just have to assign someone else who will.

Chapter 2

Thursday

Dear Diary,

Yay! Ms. Bloomberg loved my circus idea!

"I was just reading about the circus and carnival," she told us at the morning editorial meeting. "I think it would make a great subject for *The Acorn*."

In fact, Ms. Bloomberg liked my idea so much that not only am I writing about the Stars Circus and Carnival for the next issue, my article is going to be a whole two-page spread! Even Dana admitted that it would be sort of cool. I knew I was onto something with this concept!

The only person who still hated the idea was Jill.

"I really don't think this is a good idea, Ms. Bloomberg," she insisted. "Circuses can be weird. It's a strange life. You go from place to place, you never really have a home." She shook her head. "I don't think it's a good thing for students to read about. We shouldn't do an article about it."

"Look, Jill," Ms. Bloomberg told her. "If you find the circus strange, that's fine. It will give your pictures a point of view. And maybe Ashley's article can explore that part of circus life, too. She can look around and see if there's anything odd about the place."

I nodded. "Like an investigative reporter," I said.

"No, no!" Jill cried. "I didn't mean strange like that. I just meant . . . " She trailed off. Then she cleared her throat. "I just don't think it will be good for the paper, that's all."

"If you have a problem doing the piece, I can assign another photographer – " Ms. Bloomberg began.

"No, no," Jill interrupted. "I'll do it. Don't give it to anyone else, Ms. Bloomberg – please!"

Phoebe leaned in close to me. "What's up with her?" she whispered.

"I don't know," I said. "First she doesn't like the idea. Now she insists on doing it."

"Okay, Jill," Ms. Bloomberg said, a little doubtfully. "If you really want to. I'm sure it'll be a terrific piece."

"Yeah," said Jill.

But she sounded like she wasn't sure at all.

After the meeting, Ms. Bloomberg came up to me. "Ashley, I want you to help Jill," she said in a low voice. "It can be hard for a new girl to fit in, especially when she gets here in the middle of the term. You're really good at making people feel at home."

"I'll try, Ms. Bloomberg," I told her. "But she's acting kind of strange."

"She's probably just afraid that her pictures won't measure up," Ms. Bloomberg said. "But she really is good. So give her all the support you can, will you?"

I promised I would. And I will, Diary. I'm going to do my best to make sure Jill has a great time with me on this project.

I just don't understand why she doesn't seem to want to have anything to do with it. What could be so bad about a traveling circus, anyway?

Dear Diary,

It's 10:45, and I'm back in my room. I've just finished studying for my big maths exam tomorrow.

Usually, I don't worry about maths – as I've said before, I was born with a silver calculator in my mouth. But we're studying pre-algebra, and I want to get into honours algebra next year. So I'm working extra hard at it.

I was studying at a desk on the third floor of the library, where it's nice and quiet. Nobody else was around. That was good, because I was doing some really hard equations, and I wanted to focus.

All of a sudden, I heard a squeaking noise.

What could that be? I wondered. *Someone else must be up here, too.*

The squeaking sound came again.

Well, I knew that the only way I'd be able to find out what was making that sound was by getting up and checking it out. I walked along the tall bookcases.

The noise was louder now. There were some scratching, scurrying sounds, too. The back of my neck prickled. I had never noticed before how creepy the third floor could be. They keep the light low to protect the older books. It was even darker among the bookcases, away from the little lamps on the desks.

I took a breath . . . and turned the corner.

I froze. There, sitting on a shelf, was . . . was that a *rat*?

I stared at the row of shelves. Then I walked over to the rat and picked it up.

Don't worry, Diary. It wasn't a real rat. It was made of rubber. Soooooooo fake.

But I knew the *real* rat was around here somewhere! I shoved aside some American history books on the bottom shelf and found Jeremy hiding behind them. He grinned at me.

"Nice, huh?" he said, getting to his feet. "It's part of what I'm using to decorate my room for

Halloween. We're doing a sort of dungeon thing. Did I scare you?"

I shook my head. "If this was your big plan, Jeremy, it didn't work," I told him.

"Not even a little?" Jeremy asked.

I tossed the fake rat to him. "Not at all," I said. "The only thing that is scaring me right now is my maths test. It's in sixteen hours. If I hang around here with you anymore, I could fail. And *that* is *really* scary!"

"I can be scarier than any old math test," Jeremy insisted.

"Dream on," I told him. "Anyway, right now I have to study. I only have a little bit of time before curfew." I looked at my watch. "Eek!" I said. "Terrifying!"

"Very funny," Jeremy joked, sticking the rat in his backpack. As he did, a flyer for the Stars Circus and Carnival fell out.

I picked it up and handed it back to him.

He waved it at me. "Have you heard about this?"

"Sure," I told him. "As a matter of fact, Ashley is doing an article on it for *The Acorn*. We'll probably end up there a few times."

"Oh?" Jeremy said. "When are you going?"

"Probably not till Friday after school," I told him. "I've got too much homework before then."

"Maybe I'll see you there," Jeremy said.

I raised my eyebrows. "I'm surprised you want to go," I told him. "Aren't you afraid of clowns?"

Jeremy shook his head. "Who, me? No way. You must be dreaming."

"I don't think so," I said. "Didn't you hide under the seat that time we went to the Clown Around Restaurant? You know, for your birthday? When we were seven? It took Aunt Laura two hours to get you out." I giggled. "As a matter of fact, you didn't even get to blow out the candles on your – "

"Laugh all you want," Jeremy said, interrupting me. He glared over his shoulder as he turned and headed for the stairs. "You won't be laughing long. I *will* scare you this Halloween."

After Jeremy left the library, I finished studying and then went back to my room.

Campbell was already asleep.

I got into bed and pulled the covers up to my chin. But I couldn't sleep. I was too keyed up about the math test and Halloween and everything.

Which is why I pulled out a pen and a flashlight. And why I'm writing this right now.

I don't know, Diary. Jeremy is a total goof, and I'm not scared or anything. But he's clearly planning something.

I just wish I knew what it was. . . .

Chapter 3

Friday

Dear Diary,

Friday, first thing after classes, Phoebe and I picked up Mary-Kate, Campbell, and our friend Summer Sorenson. I wanted to get to the carnival as early as I could so I could look around and make some plans for my article.

Curfew wasn't until nine o'clock, so that gave us a good amount of time. We figured we could have dinner at the food stands while we were there.

"Sausage-and-pepper heroes, egg rolls, grilled sweetcorn, and lemonade – here I come!" Mary-Kate said.

"Eeew," said Summer. She wrinkled her nose. "How can you eat that stuff? It's so gross." Summer is a big health foodie.

"It *is* pretty greasy," Phoebe said, nodding.

Mary-Kate grinned. "My philosophy is, when you're at a carnival, you eat carnival food! So what are we waiting for?"

"Jill," I told her. "I need to stop by her room on the way out. I'm hoping she'll come with us. She should start checking out what she wants to photograph for the article. Plus," I added, "if she

21

has a good time with us at the carnival, she might feel better about the whole thing."

That's what I was *really* hoping for, Diary.

When we got to Jill's room – she lives in Phipps House – she was bent over a copy of *Animal Farm*. It's required reading in First Form.

"We're going to the carnival," I told her. "I thought maybe you'd want to come with us and start taking pictures. Or at least look around."

"I-I don't know," Jill said. She held up her book. "I, uh, have a lot of studying to do."

Campbell grinned. "It's Friday night. Everybody needs a little time off."

"But . . . uh . . . the flash on my camera is broken," Jill told us.

"That's okay," I said. "It will be light for a while. You can take pictures outside. Then, when your camera's fixed, you can do the indoor shots of the circus performers the next time we go."

"Well . . . " Jill hesitated for a moment. We all waited for her answer.

"Okay," she finally said.

She went over to her dresser and picked up her camera.

I smiled. "All right!"

Mary-Kate grinned. "Next stop – the fairgrounds!"

Hocus-pocus

We hurried out of the dorm and headed across the quad. I spotted Jeremy with some other Harrington boys carrying their lacrosse sticks off the field. Sometimes the boys use our grounds for practice.

Jeremy waved at us and jogged over. "Where are you going?" he asked.

"The circus," Campbell told him.

"And carnival," Summer added.

"Sounds like fun. Maybe we'll check it out, too," he said, nodding toward his friends.

"We really need to get going," I urged. I didn't want Jeremy tagging along. Besides, as fun as the carnival would be, this was a working visit.

"Okay, later!" Jeremy said. He dashed back to the other boys, and we headed off campus.

The carnival was being held on the local fairgrounds, which are right near White Oak Academy. It was about a ten-minute walk. The air was crisp, and you could smell fall in the air.

On the way, we passed the old Stone Ridge Mansion. It was a big old house on the outskirts of town that had been deserted for years. The original owners of the mansion, the Bellairs, had been very rich, and had owned all the land around for miles. In fact, the fairgrounds used to be a part of the Stone

Ridge estate. But that was a long time ago, and there were all kinds of rumours about how the Bellairs had lost their money and had to abandon the place.

There's something sort of sad about that house. It's all overgrown, with vines twining around everything. The grass is up to your knees. And the windows look like empty eyes, staring out at the quiet street.

Some of the kids at school think the house is haunted. Mary-Kate thinks that's silly. She's always telling me that there's no such thing as ghosts. But it makes me a little nervous just the same.

A few blocks after we passed the mansion, we reached the fairgrounds.

There was a big, red-and-white-striped tent pitched in the center of the field where the circus would take place. Around it, there were booths and games and rides.

"Yum!" Mary-Kate said, heading straight for the crowded food stands.

I stood on line next to Jill at the candyfloss booth. She seemed kind of distracted – she kept fiddling with her camera. When we got to the head of the line, she didn't even order anything.

Uh-oh. Was this a bad idea? I wondered. I wanted Jill to have fun at the carnival. Then she would think the article was a good idea. But she wasn't into it at all.

We joined Summer by the lemonade stand and waited for the rest of our group.

"Fried dough!" Mary-Kate said, holding up a funnel cake. "My fave!"

Phoebe and Campbell were splitting popcorn and candyfloss. "We couldn't decide," Phoebe explained, "so we figured we'd get both!"

"What should we do first?" I asked. "Jill, any ideas?"

Jill just shrugged.

"Let's work our way over to the circus tent," Mary-Kate suggested. "If anyone sees something interesting, we'll check it out."

"Sounds like a plan," Campbell said.

We wandered through the food concessions and headed toward an area with trailers and booths. The whole time Jill was frowning and keeping her eyes down. *How is she going to find things she wants to photograph if she doesn't even look up?*

I had to do something to get her into the carnival spirit.

I spotted a sign on top of a white and red trailer. "'Fortune teller,'" I read from the sign. "That looks like fun!"

25

Mary-Kate nodded. "I'm game!" she said. "Maybe we'll get some advice about our love lives."

"You don't need advice about *your* love life, Mary-Kate," said Phoebe.

She was right. Mary-Kate has been dating this really great guy named Jordan Marshall, who's at Harrington Academy for Boys.

Summer giggled. "Hey. You can never have too many boyfriends," she said. "Let's go for it."

There was a smaller sign posted outside the trailer. In red, flowery writing, it said: BETHANY PREDICTS YOUR FUTURE. KNOCK AND BE ADMITTED. FIFTY CENTS.

"Bethany is probably an old lady in a black wig and lots of makeup, with long red fingernails," Mary-Kate whispered to me.

I smiled. "Then she'll make a great character for my article," I told her.

We knocked on the trailer door.

"Come in," a voice called.

Inside, the light was dim. A bunch of lit candles were placed all around the room. They must have been scented, because it smelled very flowery in there.

There were shawls draped on a batch of chairs in a sort of waiting area. A beaded curtain hid the back of the trailer.

Hocus-pocus

"One at a time, please, girls," a voice came from behind the curtain.

"Sooooo," I said, looking at my friends. "Who should go first?"

No one said anything. I guess the atmosphere was a little more intense than we had expected.

Finally, Summer raised her hand. "I'll go!" she said.

When she came out, her eyes were shining. "I'm going to meet the cutest guy!" she told us happily. "He's an Aquarius, and he's got blonde hair and blue eyes."

Campbell rolled her eyes. "Yeah, right," she said. "I'm sure you two will be very happy together."

Campbell went in next, and came out shaking her head. "What a phony!" she whispered to me. "Do I *look* like I'm going to be thrilled to be getting a brand-new dress?"

Then it was Phoebe's turn. "Nice vintage scarf," she whispered as she came out. "And a nose ring! Didn't know too much about me, though."

I went in next, pushing aside the beaded curtain.

I had to admit, I was curious about this Bethany person.

The fortune-telling part of the trailer was pretty much like the waiting area. Lots of candles, musty scents in the air, scarves draped around. Only it was a little darker. And there was a table and two chairs in the middle of the room.

There was a girl sitting at the table.

The first thing that surprised me was how young she was. She was probably only about eighteen.

"I'm Bethany. Your name, please?" she asked.

I suddenly wanted to test her. After all, this *was* an investigative article!

"Mary-Kate," I said.

She looked up, narrowed her brown eyes, and gave me a long once-over. "No, it's not," she said. "What is your real name?"

I have to admit, Diary, I actually blushed. "Ashley," I told her.

"So. Sit down," Bethany told me, pointing to a chair.

She started shuffling a deck of cards. They weren't normal playing cards, though. They were much bigger, and they had different pictures on them.

"What are those?" I asked her.

"Tarot cards," Bethany told me. "They help me tell your fortune."

Bethany dealt some of the cards faceup in front of me and studied them. "You have a boyfriend . . . at Harrington Academy, I think."

Hocus-pocus

It was true – I really like Ross Lambert, but I wasn't too impressed with that one. Anyone who knows even a little bit about Harrington and White Oak could have guessed it.

Bethany went on to tell me some stuff about my future. I was going to do well in school this year. . . . I would have a job in fashion someday.

When she was finished and I got up to leave, she started to shuffle the cards again. "Send your sister in next," she said.

I walked through the beaded curtains. Then I froze. How did she know I have a sister? I had to admit, Diary, I was feeling a little strange.

"So how was it?" Jill asked me.

"Weird," I said, shrugging. "I didn't tell her anything about myself. Zero. Zilch. But she still knew some stuff about me. . . . "

"Oh, come on, Ashley!" Mary-Kate laughed. "She made some lucky guesses, that's all. You're not turning into a believer, are you? It's all a trick! You know that."

"Yeah," I said, nodding. "I know. So who's next?"

Mary-Kate looked at Jill. Jill shrugged. "Go ahead," she told Mary-Kate. "I don't really want to have my fortune told."

"Okay," Mary-Kate said. "Here goes nothing!"

Then Mary-Kate disappeared behind the beaded curtain.

"As soon as she's finished," I said, turning to Jill, "we can go over to the circus tent. We can take some pictures before it gets dark."

But when Mary-Kate came out, Jill decided that she wanted to get her fortune told after all. She slipped into the back room.

"All set for the circus tent?" I asked Jill when she stepped back through the beaded curtain.

She shook her head. "I think I'll take some pictures," she said. "This place is so neat, with all those candles and beads and everything." She held up her camera. "Did you want to interview Bethany?"

So while Mary-Kate, Campbell, and Summer waited outside, I interviewed Bethany. Only she didn't tell me much.

"I found that I knew what was going to happen to people before it actually happened," Bethany told me. "That's why I decided to become a fortune teller."

It sounded pretty unlikely, but I took notes anyway. She told me a little about gypsy folklore and even how she made her costumes, so I asked about her beaded top. I can't help it, Diary. I just love to know about clothes!

Hocus-pocus

The whole time, Jill kept snapping photos. The flash was a little distracting, but I was happy that she was finally interested.

She took some shots of the inside of the trailer, and of Bethany.

"You two stand next to each other," she instructed me and Bethany. Then she clicked, and the flash went off. I rubbed my eyes as little bits of light flashed in front of them.

And that's when I remembered.

Jill had told us that the flash on her camera wasn't working. But now, it seemed to be just fine.

What was up with her, anyway?

Dear Diary,

I just have to tell you about Bethany, the fortune teller at the carnival!

First surprise: When I went through the beaded curtain, there was a teenage girl sitting there – not the old lady I'd expected.

Second surprise: "You're Mary-Kate," she said in a low, husky voice.

I stared. "How did you know my name?" I demanded.

She laughed. "Your sister told me," she said. "I'm not that good. My name is Bethany, by the way."

I relaxed. Bethany actually seemed okay – turquoise nose ring and all.

I sat down, and she shuffled her cards. Tarot cards, she told me.

Then she started to talk.

"Okay. Clearly, you and Ashley are sisters." She looked up and smiled. "Although I didn't need the cards to tell me that."

She studied the cards again. "And it says here that your dad . . . your dad is some sort of professor, I think. He's back in Chicago right now. But I think there's another trip in his future . . . ."

I frowned. Bethany was right! Dad was planning a trip to Venezuela in a few months. There was a giant water bug there that he wanted to study.

You have no idea how gross it is to have a dad who studies giant water bugs. But that's a whole other story.

I have to admit, Diary. I was pretty blown away. Ashley said she didn't tell Bethany anything about us! Bethany seemed to be able to read this stuff in her tarot cards . . . and she was totally on target!

Bethany stared down at the last card on the table. "This is your future," she said. "Your immediate future, anyway."

She bit her lip and narrowed her eyes at me. "Mary-Kate, you should go play a game at the carnival. Go-Fish, I think.

"And while you're there," she went on, her hands hovering just above the cards, "watch for a guy . . . ." She looked at the cards again. Her voice was kind of dreamy. "A guy in a red T-shirt. He's going to give you something."

Bethany stared at the cards for another minute. Then she looked up. "That's it," she said cheerfully. "That's all I can see for now."

"Well, thanks," I said, handing her my fifty cents.

"I've got to tell you something," Bethany said as I stood up. "You're an amazing subject, Mary-Kate. You're so open!

"Few people have as clear a spirit as you do," she went on. "You really should come back sometime and do this again. And if you do, it's free."

"Uh, yeah. Sure," I told her. "Thanks a lot."

I left Bethany and went back to my friends.

"So? So?" Campbell said. "A total waste of time, right?"

"What did she say, Mary-Kate?" Ashley asked. "You look kind of funny."

I shrugged. "No biggie," I told them.

But I have to admit, I wasn't telling the exact truth.

33

I mean, I don't believe in this stuff, Diary – not at all.

But how could Bethany have known so much about Dad?

Anyway, I decided to play Go-Fish – just to see what would happen. So after my sister interviewed Bethany and Jill took some pictures, I dragged everyone over to the arcade games.

The Go-Fish booth is the one where they have little plastic fishes in the water, and they give you a rod with a bobby pin on the end of it and you have to catch three fish to win.

"We're going to make a lemonade run," Campbell said.

"Okay," I said. "I'm going to stick with the game." I didn't want to tell them I was waiting to see if Bethany's prediction would come true. I felt too silly.

"Meet you back here in a few." Campbell, Summer, and Phoebe took off. Ashley scribbled in her notebook, while I played Go-Fish. Jill played, too. She was pretty good at it. But, Diary – I lost every game! I was too busy looking around.

I glimpsed a red shirt in a crowd heading my way. *Is that him?* I wondered. *What's he going to give me?*

Then the crowd parted and I saw that it wasn't a *boy* in the red shirt, it was a short woman!

I shook my head. *It's not going to happen*, I told myself. *Forget it.* I clutched the fishing rod and tried snagging another fish.

Then a tall guy in a red T-shirt ran toward me! My heart pounded. *Is it going to happen?* I held my breath. *Nope!* He kept right on running.

Get a grip, I ordered myself.

Summer, Campbell, and Phoebe came back with their lemonade. Suddenly, Ashley poked me. "Oh, no!" she whispered. "It's Jeremy – the biggest pain in the universe. Let's get out of here!"

But Jeremy had seen us already. He headed straight for us. He was carrying a giant stuffed bear in his arms.

"I was hoping to see you – not!" he said to Ashley. Then he turned to me. "So, Mary-Kate," he said, raising his eyebrows. "Win anything yet?"

"Nah," I said, "but if you let me get back to Go-Fishing, maybe I will."

Suddenly, he thrust the big stuffed bear into my arms. He almost made me drop my fishing rod. "If the guys see me with this, I'll never hear the end of it," he told me. "Besides, this same carnival was in my roommate's town a few weeks

35

ago. I won so much stuff, I have no place to put anything else."

I stared at him, surprised. This was the nicest thing he had done for me in a long time. "Thanks," I said finally.

"Yeah, sure," he replied, and walked away, whistling.

I stared after him. Then, I blinked. There was something I hadn't noticed before.

"He's wearing a RED T-SHIRT!" I cried.

I looked down at the bear in my arms. "Take it, Ashley!" I said, shoving it at my sister.

"Sure," she said, taking the stuffed bear. She stared at me. "What's the matter, Mary-Kate? You look like you've seen a ghost!"

And that's when I told my friends about what Bethany had said, Diary. About how a guy in a red T-shirt was going to give me something at the Go-Fish booth.

"And it happened just like Bethany said it would?" Summer shook her head. "Wow. Cosmic."

"She told me I should come back, too," I added. "She said I had a great aura or something. That it was easy to tell my future."

"Oh, come on," Campbell scoffed. The rest of them didn't say a word.

The whole thing was . . . well, almost creepy.

Hocus-pocus

"Look, you guys," Campbell said briskly. "Time for some rides. There's a seat on the Terminator with my name on it!"

I knew she just wanted to get our minds off the spooky thing that had just happened. And you know what, Diary? She had the right idea!

For the next hour or so, we went on all the rides in the carnival. I've always loved rides – the wilder, the better. I screamed my head off. By the time we were done, we had to race back to school. Curfew was in fifteen minutes.

Ashley was a little upset. It was too late to go to the circus, and she had wanted to scout it out for her article.

"Don't worry," I told her. "I'll come back with you tomorrow. I want to see Bethany one more time, anyway."

"You want to see the fortune teller again?" Ashley said, starring at me.

I have to admit, I was surprised myself. I never would have predicted it, Diary. (Get it? *Predicted* it? Well, *I* thought it was pretty funny!) But I was curious about Bethany and what she had said.

On the way home, we passed the old Stone Ridge Mansion again. Now that it was dark out, it was even spookier.

"That place creeps me out," Phoebe said. "Especially at night. Every time I pass by, I feel like it's looking at me."

"Me, too," said Summer. "Did you know it's supposed to be haunted? There's a story about a sad little girl who holds a lantern in the window."

"Come on," Campbell said, shaking her head. "You don't really believe in ghosts, do you?"

Summer shivered. "I don't know. I mean, I sort of do. I mean . . . oh, I don't know what I mean!"

"How about you, Jill?" Campbell asked.

Jill shook her head. "I think it's a beautiful old house. It just needs someone to pay attention to it. Clean it up and take care of it. I was thinking of taking some photographs of it someday."

I glanced at the house. It almost looked like a movie set – for an old-fashioned scary movie.

Who had lived there? I wondered. *Were they happy? Sad? What had happened behind those windows, anyway?*

And is it haunted, like people say it is?

Chapter 4

Saturday

Dear Diary,

The strangest thing just happened. I went to pick up Jill so that we could go back and see the circus. When I got to her room, her door was open, so I stuck my head inside.

But there was no Jill! Instead, there were two grown-ups sitting on her bed.

"Uh, hi," I said, stepping into the room. "I was just looking for Jill. Have you seen her?"

The woman got up. "You must be Ashley!" she said, smiling. She wore a simple blue dress, and kind of reminded me of a kindergarten teacher. "Jill has told us all about you. I'm Jill's mother. And this is her father. We're glad to meet you."

Jill's dad was in a grey suit and a thin, red tie. He looked like a businessman.

Just then, Jill came back into the room. "Ashley!" she said. She seemed surprised to see me. "You've met my parents. Well, let's go."

"We don't have to leave just yet," I said. "I don't want to interrupt your visit."

I turned to Jill's parents. "My dad is always travelling," I told them. "So when he comes to visit, my sister, Mary-Kate, and I want to spend as much time with him as we can."

"You have a sister – " Jill's mom started to ask.

But Jill cut her off. "Yeah, Ashley has a sister," she told them.

Then she turned to me. "My mom and dad have been here for a while," she said. "It's okay. Really.

"We have to go," she told her parents. "To the circus. There's that article I told you about. . . ."

"We understand," her dad said. He stood up. "It's nice meeting you, Ashley. Hope to see you again."

It was a little strange. I mean, Jill's parents were perfectly nice, but Jill seemed to want to get rid of them as soon as possible.

Oh, well. I guess you never know about a person's relationship with her parents. Mary-Kate and I are kind of spoiled in that way. Dad is so great!

Anyway, Jill and I had an excellent morning at the carnival. Her camera was working fine, and she took some terrific shots. I interviewed some of the people who worked the concession booths.

"I bet I can get some good shots here," Jill said. She led me to a tent where there were a lot of different acts. A face-painter was putting makeup on little kids, while a woman twisted balloons into animal shapes. There was even a sword swallower and a bearded lady – just like in an old-fashioned circus! The bearded lady let me pull on her beard, and Jill got a picture of it. It's going to look great in *The Acorn*!

Then it was time to go to the afternoon performance of the circus.

Jill looked a little worried. The closer we got to the circus tent, the more nervous she seemed to get.

"Is everything okay?" I asked.

"What?" She looked startled. "Oh, yeah. Fine." She smiled at me, but I didn't quite believe that nothing was bothering her.

Even if she was having some kind of problem being there, she was still a total pro. She kept snapping away.

The show was really great. "My hands hurt from clapping so hard," I told Jill. She just nodded and shot some more pictures.

"Cool!" I said as two clowns bounded into the ring. "I love clowns!"

The circus had five clowns, but the funniest of them all were a man and a woman who played a married couple. The woman was cleaning her "house" when the man came home.

Wherever he went, she cleaned. She accidentally dusted his head and made him sneeze. She shook out a rug he was standing on and sent him flying. She scared him with the vacuum cleaner, which seemed to turn into a kind of snake as she used it. She even dumped a pail of water over his head.

Through it all, he was sweet and patient and silly. I've never laughed so hard in my life.

"I can't wait to interview them!" I whispered to Jill after they had left the arena.

"Interview them?" Jill said. "Oh, I don't know. Do you really want to interview some clowns?"

"Why not?" I asked, getting up to leave. "They were the best part of the show!"

"Yeah," Jill said. "But all the magic disappears when they take off their makeup, you know? It's all about make-believe. It would ruin things to see them without their noses and stuff."

"Then we should talk to them before they take off their makeup," I told her. "Let's go. The dressing rooms are right over there!"

That's when Jill grabbed my arm. "Ashley!" she cried. "Come *on*!"

Diary, she actually dragged me out of the tent!

Jill was acting totally strange. I just didn't get her. And all because I wanted to interview a pair of clowns.

Then I had it – an Ashley brainstorm!

Hocus-pocus

I knew why Jill was so uncomfortable at the circus. Why she didn't want to go backstage to meet the clowns. Why she wanted to nix the whole circus concept from the start.

Jill must be scared of clowns – just like my cousin Jeremy!

"Look, Jill," I told her. "If you're . . . well . . . nervous around the clowns, I understand. My cousin Jeremy has been scared of clowns ever since he was little. Lots of people are. It's nothing to be ashamed of. . . ."

"Scared of clowns?" she gasped. "Scared of them? Well . . . I guess . . . I am, sort of."

"Maybe I can help," I offered.

But Jill shook her head. "Believe me, Ashley," she said, "there's absolutely nothing you can do about it."

What is it with Jill? One minute, she's nice and quiet and perfectly okay. The next, she's – oh, I don't know, Diary, just plain *weird*.

Dear Diary,

Okay, okay. I know what you're going to say, Diary (that is, if you could talk). Fortune telling is not for real. It's all a trick.

43

Even so, I went back to talk to Bethany again.

I couldn't help it. After all, she predicted *everything* that happened the other day! The present, the guy, the red T-shirt. It wasn't her fault that the guy was Jeremy.

So this morning, I walked over to the fairgrounds with Ashley and Jill.

They had lots of stuff to do for their article, so I just wandered around by myself, eating fried dough and watching people go on the rides. I spent a dollar and tossed a few balls in one of the basketball hoops. None went in. I wondered how Jeremy had managed to win all those prizes. It's not as easy as it looks!

Thinking about Jeremy, of course, made me think about the red T-shirt again.

And that made me think about Bethany.

Could she really predict the future?

Well, there was only one way to find out.

I walked over to her trailer and went in.

"Mary-Kate!" Bethany greeted me with a smile. "I'm so glad you came back! Sit down."

Bethany took out her tarot cards and placed five of them on the table. "Hmm," she said. "This is interesting."

"What's interesting?" I asked.

44

Hocus-pocus

"Look here," Bethany said, pointing to a card. "Somebody is going to give you a present. And it looks like something you really want."

"Not another stuffed animal, huh?" I asked.

"I don't know," she said. "But the cards say you're going to be receiving a present from someone very soon."

I shook my head. It wasn't my birthday. And Christmas was two months away. Who would give me a present?

Anyway, that was all that Bethany saw. She told me I was welcome anytime.

After I left her, I went back to the dorm.

And *that*, Diary, is when things really got weird.

When I arrived, Phoebe and Ginger Halliday – she was my roommate for a while – were hanging out in my room with Campbell. Ginger and Campbell have always been close.

As I flopped down on my bed, Campbell went over to her desk and picked up an envelope. "This is for you, Mary-Kate," she said. "It showed up an hour ago. Somebody stuck it under the door."

I took the envelope and opened it. Inside were two tickets to the New Hampshire College women's basketball finals, featuring my favorite team: the Hampshire Hoops!

The game was totally sold out. The tickets were impossible to get. And suddenly I had two of them!

"Incredible!" Campbell exclaimed. "Who sent them?"

I looked in the envelope for a note, but there was nothing else in it. I looked at the outside of the envelope. My name was printed on it in block letters. But there was no return address.

That's when I remembered Bethany. "I can't believe it," I said. "She predicted this would happen!"

"Who?" Phoebe wanted to know.

"Bethany," I told her. "I went back to the carnival today. She said I'd be getting a gift. And here it is."

"But how could she have known?" Ginger said, tucking a bright red curl behind an ear.

I stared at the tickets. "I have no idea. And who could have sent them, anyway? They sold out a week ago!"

"Who cares?" Campbell said. "The real question is, who are you going to take?" She smiled sweetly at me.

I smiled back. "You, of course," I said. "After all, you're the only person I know who's a bigger fan than I am."

"Yay!" Campbell jumped up and down. "Thank you, Mary-Kate, thank you thank you thank you. This is so cool."

"We've just got to go back to see this Bethany person again," Ginger said.

"Go back? Why?" I asked.

"So that I can get my fortune told!" Ginger exclaimed. "I can't believe I didn't go with you the first time!"

"I want mine done again, too," Phoebe added. "I'm going to write down all the questions I want to ask." She took a piece of paper from my desk.

Campbell turned to me. "You know, it's not such a bad idea," she said. "I mean, you know I don't believe in this stuff. But I have to admit – Bethany seems to know what she's talking about. So we should ask her as many questions as we can. She's only going to be here for a few more days."

Campbell had a point. After all, Bethany was about to disappear. I might as well find out everything I could before she left.

That's when I remembered what I had said to Jeremy.

I had told him I didn't believe in any of this supernatural stuff.

Had I been wrong?

Chapter 5

Monday

Dear Diary,

You are totally not going to believe what happened today. I hardly believe it myself – and I'm the one it happened to!

After classes were over, Campbell, Phoebe, Ginger, and I went back to the carnival to see Bethany.

Ashley couldn't come with me this time. "I'm going to do some studying," she told me after class. "I need to catch up on my homework. It feels like I spent the whole weekend at the carnival."

"Is Jill okay with the article now?" I asked.

Ashley shrugged. "I think so," she said. "She's been taking some amazing pictures. But she seems really freaked out by the circus." Ashley leaned closer. "I think she might be afraid of clowns," she said quietly.

"Just like Jeremy!" we said in unison. Sometimes that happens to us. It's a sister thing, I guess.

"Yeah." Ashley sighed. "I'll probably have to go interview the clowns by myself. But when I mention doing that, Jill freaks out even more. I just don't get it."

"You will," I told my sister. "Everyone always confides in you, Ashley. Jill will open up. Just give her a little more time."

"I hope you're right," said Ashley. "The carnival won't be here after Halloween."

"Then it won't be a problem anymore," I told her.

She nodded. "That's true," she said. "But I'd still like to find out what's going on."

We got to the carnival at about 3:30. This time, we all had our lists of questions for Bethany. After all, as Phoebe said, "We might as well know what to ask her."

And this time, I went first.

I have to admit, I had a ton of things I wanted to find out: What will I be when I grow up? Does Jordan really like me? Are the Mighty Oaks going to win this year's softball championship? (I'm playing first base.)

"Hold it, hold it!" Bethany said, shaking her head and smiling. "Let me finish dealing the cards, Mary-Kate.

"Look," she continued. "There's a lot I can't see, because it's too far in the future. With Jordan, well . . . it looks good – at least for the next year or so. After that, it gets murky. But there's something" – Bethany turned over another card – "something that has to do with numbers. With maths. I'm seeing the number ninety-four. Does that number mean anything to you?"

I thought hard. "Nope."

"Have you had any tests lately?" Bethany asked.

"Yes!" I said, remembering my math test. I had taken it on Friday. But Mr. Geller, my math teacher, hadn't given the tests back yet. "Could ninety-four be my grade?"

"It might be," Bethany said.

After everyone else had their turns, we all headed back to White Oak.

"I don't know," said Ginger. "She didn't say very much to me."

"She told me I was going into fashion design." Campbell snorted, looking down at her scuffed sneakers, jeans, and – what else? – her Boston Red Sox T-shirt. "I seriously doubt that."

"She said something to me about the number ninety-four," I said. "When are we getting our maths tests back? Tomorrow?"

"I think so," said Phoebe. "But you could e-mail Mr. Geller. He'll tell you."

So I did, Diary. And Mr. Geller e-mailed me right back.

Now here's what you're not going to believe.

Hocus-pocus

He said we were getting our test scores back tomorrow, but that I had nothing to worry about.

I had gotten a 94!!!

Bethany had guessed the exact right number. What were the chances of that?

Somehow, everything that she's predicting is coming true.

Bethany has got to be the real deal. I can feel it!

I can't wait to tell Ashley!

Dear Diary,

I had a big fight with Mary-Kate. We made up at the end of it, of course. We always do.

But I'm getting seriously worried.

Mary-Kate came over just as I was finishing a draft of my article. She was really excited.

"Ashley, you're not going to believe it!" she told me. "I got a ninety-four on my math test!!"

"What's not to believe?" I said, giving her a hug. "You're a whiz in math. Congratulations."

"No, no, it's not that." Mary-Kate shook her head. "Bethany predicted it! She predicted that I'd get a ninety-four! She is totally for real!"

"What are you talking about?" I asked her.

So Mary-Kate told me all about how she had gone back to the carnival, and that Bethany "saw" her grade in those tarot cards she uses.

I have to tell you, Diary, she really freaked me out.

"Look, Mary-Kate," I told her. "Remember when I was reading about Harry Houdini? He was the greatest magician who ever lived.

"But he didn't believe in magic," I went on. "In fact, Houdini spent most of his life trying to prove that people like Bethany are just tricking you."

"Why are you so sure she is?" Mary-Kate demanded. "There's so much stuff she's told me that's come true!"

"And there's so much she's told everybody else that hasn't," I reminded her.

"Yeah," Mary-Kate said. "But Bethany says I'm special."

"I *know* you are," I told her. "Mary-Kate, you're the most special sister anyone could have. I'm just not sure you're special in *this* way."

That's when Mary-Kate got mad at me.

She told me I had a closed mind. That dad has always said that you need to formulate a hypothesis and test it out. And that Bethany was testing out fine.

I knew I couldn't get her to see it my way. So I just told her I was sorry. Then she told me she was sorry. So I guess it ended okay.

I have to admit, though, I honestly don't think Bethany is on the level. I don't think anyone can predict the future.

But that would mean that something even worse could be going on. Could Bethany be trying to trick Mary-Kate in some way?

I am so mixed up!

I do know one thing, though: From now on, when I'm at the carnival, I'm keeping an eye on Bethany.

Chapter 6

Tuesday

Dear Diary,

Campbell and I had the greatest time last night!

We went to the basketball game with my mysterious tickets – and the Hampshire Hoops won! I even got the autographs of the five starters. It was awesome.

Then, this afternoon, Campbell and I went back to the carnival with Ginger and Summer. I wanted to thank Bethany for the tickets. But I also figured she might have something else to tell me. After all, she's going to be leaving town right after Halloween. I wanted to get all the info I could before she was gone.

"This is interesting," Bethany said after she laid out the cards. Her dark eyes twinkled. "I think you're going to like this prediction."

"Really?" I said, leaning over the table and peering at the cards. "What do you see?"

"Three different boys are going to call you. They are going to ask you for dates."

"You're kidding," I said.

She shook her head. "And none of them will be your boyfriend, Jordan."

How about *that*, Diary? She even knew Jordan's name.

"Dream on, Bethany!" Campbell laughed when I told her what Bethany had said.

"What?" I said. "You don't think it's possible that three guys might be interested in me?"

"Time out!" Campbell said, throwing up her hands. "I didn't mean that, Mary-Kate! Thousands of guys are interested in you, I'm sure. It's just, well . . . "

I smiled. "I know. I was just kidding. It *is* pretty unlikely."

Summer sighed. "She told me I was going to meet someone tall, dark, and handsome."

"The last time you went, she said you'd meet a blonde and blue-eyed guy, didn't she?" Campbell pointed out.

"Did she?" Summer said, and laughed. "Well, maybe I'm going to be dating two guys at the same time!"

As we left the trailer, I saw my cousin Jeremy waiting on line to go in.

"You? Seeing a fortune teller?" I said, and raised my eyebrows. "I didn't think you believed in this stuff."

"Well . . . I . . . " Jeremy leaned in toward me and lowered his voice. "Look, don't tell any of the guys, okay? But I heard that this Bethany person was really on the mark, you know?"

"We won't breathe a word to a soul," I reassured him. "Anyway, she's been pretty on target with me. Remember that stuffed bear you gave me?"

"Yeah," Jeremy said. "What about it?"

"Well, Bethany predicted that would happen," I told him.

Jeremy shook his head. "Mary-Kate," he said, rolling his eyes, "if I'd known you were going to get so goofy about that bear, I never would have given it to you in the first place."

"She also predicted that you would be wearing a red T-shirt," I told him.

"Don't get weird on me," Jeremy warned.

"Who's the weird one in this family?" I said. "Don't even get me started."

"Okay," Jeremy said, holding up his hand. "I won't."

He walked up the steps of Bethany's trailer. Then he ducked inside.

I wonder what Bethany will see in the cards for Jeremy? I thought.

That made me think about what Bethany had predicted for me. Three guys asking me out . . . on the same night?

Hocus-pocus

It would never, ever happen.

Yup! This time, I was sure that Bethany had finally blown it.

Dear Diary,

Jill and I were at the fair today, doing some last-minute interviews before we handed in the first draft of our article.

As we passed Bethany's trailer, my cousin Jeremy was there, too! I have to admit that really surprised me. I mean, guys don't usually go for that fortune telling stuff.

I must have had a funny expression on my face, because Jill asked me if there was anything wrong.

"It's my sister and that fortune teller," I told her. "I'm really getting worried. Mary-Kate is actually starting to believe her."

"What's so terrible about that?" Jill asked. "I don't believe in fortune telling. But if Mary-Kate wants to . . . "

"What if she gets hurt?" I asked Jill. "What if Bethany tells her that something great is going to happen, and Mary-Kate really wants it to, and it doesn't?"

"Well, then she'll be disappointed," Jill said gently. "But that's the best way to convince her that the whole thing is a fake – isn't it?"

"It *is* a fake, right?" I pushed my hair out of my eyes. "I mean, this whole carnival is a lot of fun, but you shouldn't take it seriously, right? I bet lots of the workers here are probably just scamming people – "

I stopped. Jill's mouth was hanging open in astonishment. She stared at me as if I had said something terrible.

"It's not like that, Ashley!" she protested. "Not at all! I mean, I don't believe that Bethany is the real thing," she went on. "But most of the people here are artists, doing what they love. They're just like the people in the great circuses. They're really good at what they do, and the circus is the only place they can do it!"

Listening to Jill, I started to get so excited that I stopped worrying about Mary-Kate for a few minutes.

"You know, that's a great angle for our article!" I told her. "The dedicated artists of the Stars Circus and Carnival!"

"It might work," Jill said slowly.

Just then, one of the clowns left the circus tent. He was walking toward us. "Hi, Jill!" he said as he passed.

Jill looked over at him. Then she quickly looked away.

It wasn't until a few minutes later that I realised something. We haven't even had a chance to talk to any of the clowns yet . . . mostly because Jill seems incredibly so freaked out by them.

So how did the clown know Jill's name?

Chapter 7

Wednesday

Dear Diary,

Weirder and weirder and weirder. That's how things are around here these days!

It all started around seven o'clock. Campbell and I had just come back from the dining hall when the phone rang.

She picked it up and listened for a second. Then she handed it to me. "It's for you, Mary-Kate," she said. "Some guy named Mark."

I took the phone and said hello.

"Uh, Mary-Kate?" a guy said on the other end. "My name is Mark Greene. I'm in the First Form at Harrington. You don't know me. But I've, uh, seen you around. I was wondering if you might want to go out with me."

"Are you sure you don't want my sister, Ashley?" I asked him. "We look a lot alike."

"No," said Mark. "I asked some guys, and they told me you were Mary-Kate. I mean, I know you're Mary-Kate. I mean – "

I smiled. "I know what you mean," I told him.

"So," he went on. "What do you say? Will you go out with me?"

"Uh, gee, Mark," I said, as Campbell made goofy faces at me. "I'm sorry. But I'm seeing somebody right now."

"Oh. All right, then," Mark said. "Thanks, anyway." Then he hung up.

"What was that about?" Campbell demanded.

"Oh, a guy. Asking me out," I said. I stared at the phone. *Did that really just happen?*

"Who was he?" Campbell said.

"I don't know," I told her, feeling sort of flattered. "That's what makes it weird. He seemed to know who I am, though."

Then the phone rang again.

This time, *I* picked it up.

"Hello?" a guy's voice said. "Is this Mary-Kate Burke?"

"Yes, it is," I answered.

"This is Robbie Morris," the voice said.

"Okay . . . " I said. "Do I know you?"

"Uh, no," he said. "I go to Harrington, though." He cleared his throat nervously. "I wanted to know if you're busy on Saturday night."

"Really?" I asked.

"Well, yeah," Robbie said.

"I'm sorry," I told him. "I'm seeing somebody." Then I thought of something. "Who gave you my number – "

But Robbie Morris had already hung up.

"How strange is *that*?" I said, shaking my head. "Another guy wanting to ask me out."

I looked at Campbell. She looked at me.

"Bethany!" we both said at once.

I took several steps away from the phone. Her prediction was really coming true! My heart beat a little faster. This was definite proof that her fortune telling was real.

"Oh, come on," Campbell said, her voice a little shaky. "It's a coincidence. Right? It has to be!"

The phone rang again.

We both just looked at it.

It kept ringing. Finally, Campbell picked it up. "Yeah? Yeah?" she said. "Okay." She hung up and smiled.

"Who was it?" I asked nervously.

"Just Phoebe," Campbell said. "We're going to study together later."

I nodded.

Okay. Two guys had asked me out on a date tonight.

There's nothing strange about that, right? Maybe the guys at Harrington finally noticed how great I am.

Hocus-pocus

I shook my head, sat down at my desk, and started on my history homework. *This is just silly*, I told myself. *Total coincidence.*

The phone rang again.

I stared at it as though it were a poisonous snake.

Campbell made a grab for it, but I stopped her. "Don't," I said. "This is too weird."

It rang and rang. Then it stopped ringing.

I breathed a sigh of relief.

It rang again.

"All right already!" I yelled, and grabbed it. "Hello?" I said.

"It's . . . uh . . . Danny Lewin. From Harrington. Is this Mary-Kate?"

"Yes," I said. Campbell raised her eyebrows. I nodded.

"I'm a friend of someone you know," he said. "I was wondering if you'd like to go out with me."

"No, thank you," I said, my voice shaking a little. "I already have a boyfriend."

"Right," he said quickly, and hung up.

I sat down on my bed. My heart was pounding. Bethany told me this would happen – and it did! I was scared and excited at the same time.

Campbell went over to the bookshelves and pulled out the Harrington student guide.

"What are you doing?" I asked her.

"I want to see if any of these guys are for real," she told me.

Well, Diary, each of the boys who had called really was a student at Harrington. None of them were anywhere near as cute as Jordan. But, I had to admit, they weren't total losers, either.

And Bethany had predicted the whole thing.

Clearly, I had to go back and talk to her again.

So I did . . . the very next day after school.

This time, when Bethany looked at my tarot cards, she frowned. I could tell something was bothering her.

The back of my neck prickled. So far, everything she had predicted was good. Was that about to change?

"Listen, Mary-Kate," she said. Her husky voice was serious. "Is there a deserted house in town?" She shut her eyes as if she were concentrating really hard. "Is it called something like . . . Rock Hill? Stone something?"

I gasped. "Stone Ridge," I said. "The old Stone Ridge Mansion?"

Bethany nodded. She studied the cards again. "On Halloween eve, you should go there," she told me. "And take your sister, too."

"Why?" I asked.

"I can't quite tell," said Bethany, shaking her head. "But someone there wants to communicate with you . . . with you and your sister. She's going to . . . to . . . give you something. Some sort of treasure that she's been hiding there for a long, long time."

"What do you mean? Who is she?" I asked.

Bethany closed her eyes. Then she opened them again and looked at me. "I'm sorry," she said. "The images have faded."

This time, Bethany's prediction kind of freaked me out. But I knew what I had to do.

When I got back to school, I went to find Ashley. "You've got to come to the mansion with me," I told her.

"No way," she said. "You know how I feel about this stuff."

"Ashley, please," I begged. "Everything Bethany told me so far has come true. Maybe . . . maybe there really is a ghost who needs to communicate with us or something."

"A *ghost*?" Ashley stared at me. "I thought you didn't believe in ghosts."

"I don't," I told her. "But Bethany said – -"

"Bethany said?" Ashley sighed. "Mary-Kate – "

"Pretty please?" I said. "Ashley, you're my sister.

You're not going to make me go there alone, are you?"

"Well, if you put it that way," Ashley said grumpily. Then she smiled. "But I'm just standing in front of the house," she said. "No way I'm going inside. Somebody owns that place, and we would be trespassing."

"You got it," I told her. "Just in front. We won't even stay very long. And Ashley?"

"What?"

"Thanks!"

And, Diary, I meant that thank-you with my whole heart!

Dear Diary,

Okay. It's official. My sister has flipped. But more about that later.

First, let me tell you what happened with Jill. It is truly amazing.

Remember the other day, when the clown called her by name? When we got back to school, I asked her about it. "What was up with that clown?" I asked.

"What clown?" Jill replied.

"The one who knew your name," I said.

"I don't know what you're talking about," she said, looking away.

Believe me, Diary, I know what I heard. But I

decided not to argue with her. Not then, anyway.
The first draft of my article was due on Thursday,
and I was determined to interview the clowns
before I handed it in.

So I went back to the circus this afternoon, after
classes. By myself. I took my own camera. I didn't
want to upset Jill, but I really wanted pictures to go
with the article.

It was just before the show, and the clowns were
in their dressing room.

I knocked.

"Come in!" somebody said.

I opened the door.

And there, sitting in the dressing room, were . . .
Jill's mom and dad!

"Excuse me," I said, completely confused. "I'm
looking for the clowns. . . ."

That's when I noticed what was on the dressing
table, in addition to the red noses, wigs, and lots of
clown makeup.

There, sitting in a gold frame, were two pictures.
One was of a little girl, in clown makeup, with two
clowns. They were hugging.

The other was a picture of *Jill*.

I suddenly realized something. "You . . . you're
those two clowns!" I said. "The really funny

ones!"

"Yes," Jill's mom said. "Thank you, Ashley. I'm glad you like our act."

That's when Jill rushed into the room. "Mom – " she started to say.

Then she saw me.

"Your parents are clowns?" I asked her.

Jill just stared at me. Then she turned and ran out of the dressing room.

"Jill!" her father called. He raced out after her.

I was speechless. And I'm sure you know, Diary, that I'm not usually at a loss for words.

Why had Jill run away?

Are her parents really clowns?

And if they are, why hadn't she told me?

Chapter 8

Saturday, Halloween Eve

Dear Diary,

So, Diary, it turned out that the reason Jill didn't want me to meet the clowns was that the clowns are her parents!

After Jill ran out of the dressing room, her mom turned to me. "Ashley," she said, "I'm so sorry. Jill wanted us to keep this a secret from all the girls at White Oak."

"But, why?" I asked. "I think the fact that you're clowns is totally amazing!"

Mrs. Jenkins smiled slightly. "Thanks, dear," she said. "But, you see, Jill doesn't.

"When she was little," Mrs. Jenkins went on, "she loved that we were clowns. We could always make her laugh. And we made her the best birthday parties. All the people from the circus would come. . . ."

Mrs. Jenkins voice trailed off as she looked at Jill's photo. "Jill always went to boarding schools," she explained. "She had to, because we traveled so much. Last year, some girls at her old school were very mean to her.

"They started teasing her about our jobs. Their parents were doctors and lawyers and business owners. Suddenly, having clowns in the family was embarrassing to Jill.

"So we put her in White Oak Academy," Mrs. Jenkins said. "And decided to keep our profession a secret."

"It must have been hard when you came to town," I said.

"Yes, it was." Mrs. Jenkins sighed. "But we thought it would be okay. After all, when we're working, we're always in full clown makeup. Nobody would recognize us. We would have probably gotten away with it . . . "

"Until I decided to write the article," I said, nodding.

"Yes," Mrs. Jenkins said. "After we met you the first time, I had the feeling you'd figure things out sooner or later."

"I just want you to know," I said, "that I think it's awesome you're clowns."

"So do we, Ashley," Mrs. Jenkins said. "I can't think of anything I'd rather do. Making kids laugh. . . " Mrs. Jenkins' eyes lit up. "It's the best feeling in the world."

"Would you mind telling me more about it?" I asked her. "It would really be great to write about in my article."

"Of course," said Mrs. Jenkins. She stared into space for a moment, as if she was remembering the past. "I always knew I wanted to join the circus," she began. "Even though my parents didn't approve.

"So after I went to college, when I was twenty-one years old, I went to Florida. There used to be a special clown college there . . . ." Jill's parent met at the clown college. It sounded like an incredible place.

We talked for a long time. Then she let me try on one of her wigs.

A half hour later, when Jill came back with her dad, I was in full clown makeup. I had a bright yellow wig on my head. My face was painted white. I had red lips, black-rimmed eyes, and a blue tear on my right cheek. And my eyebrows were pointy, so I had a kind of surprised expression.

"It's amazing how it transforms you," Mrs. Jenkins was telling me as I looked in the mirror. "It's almost impossible to tell who you are under there. I think that's what really frees you up to be silly in front of a crowd."

I turned to Jill. "Jill, this is so cool and so much fun! I love that your parents are clowns. And if it's okay with you," I went on, "I think we should feature them in our article."

"But if everybody at school finds out, what will they think?" Jill groaned. She sank down onto a cot.

"They'll think it's really neat." I went over and sat beside her. "Look. Maybe the kids at your old school made fun of you because your parents are clowns. But the girls at White Oak aren't like that. I promise! They're going to think this is the most awesome thing ever!

"Besides," I went on, "your mom just promised me that I can be in tomorrow's show as a clown! I won't do it unless you think it's okay. But I really want to."

"You do?" Jill said, amazed. "You *want* to be a clown?"

"You bet!" I told her. "Are you kidding? To have a chance to perform in a real circus? This is the most exciting thing that's ever happened to me!"

Just then, Mary-Kate poked her head inside the dressing room. "Jill?" she said, glancing around. "Have you seen Ashley? I thought she was with you."

"Mary-Kate? It's me!" I said, laughing.

"What?" Mary-Kate looked at me. She looked again. Then her eyes lit up. "You're kidding! That's really you in there?"

"Absolutely," I said.

Hocus-pocus

"Wow." Mary-Kate looked at me and laughed. "I knew you liked makeup, Ashley, but I never thought you'd go this far!"

She sat down on one of the chairs at the makeup table. "Can I try some on, too?" she asked Jill's mom.

Mrs. Jenkins smiled. "Be our guest!"

In ten minutes, Mary-Kate was also in full clown makeup. And Mr. Jenkins promised her that we *both* could be in tomorrow's show.

Jill stood there, looking completely confused.

Mary-Kate glanced at her in the mirror. "Are you going to be in the show, too?" she asked.

"Me?" Jill said.

"Yeah!" Mary-Kate said. "Why not? Don't you want to be?"

"Well, I-I guess so," Jill began.

Mary-Kate grabbed my hand. "Ashley!" she said. "We've got to invite all our friends! They are going to be so jealous!"

I looked over at Jill. She was beginning to smile.

I smiled back at her.

I finally understood why Jill was "afraid" of clowns.

She was really afraid of kids making fun of her.

But those kids weren't her friends anymore.

We are!

Dear Diary,

Tonight is the night Ashley and I are going to visit the Stone Ridge Mansion. I have to find out who – or what – has something to give us, and what it is.

We decided to head over just after dinner.

"Hey. I'll go, too," Campbell offered. "What are friends for?"

"Count me in," said Phoebe.

Summer was too scared, but Ginger decided to come. And so did Jill. After what had happened with her parents, she really started to relax with us and open up. She took her camera, just in case there was anything to photograph.

"We have about an hour before curfew," I said as we left the dorm.

"It only takes five minutes to get there," Campbell said. "That'll be plenty of time."

"Way more than enough time," Phoebe said nervously.

It was already dark out, and we all carried flashlights. The night air was crisp and cool. I shivered a little.

"Scared, are you?" said Campbell

"No way!" I told her. "I'm just a little chilly. I should have worn a heavier sweater."

But I was a *little* scared.

A few minutes later, we were standing in the front yard of the mansion. We crept up the path until we were about twenty feet away from the front door. The house looked dark and deserted.

There were a few homes across the street with lights in some of the windows. "We can always run over there if we need help," Ashley said. She sounded nervous.

"We're not going to need any help," I told her, sounding braver than I felt.

"Now what do we do?" whispered Ginger.

"I don't know," I told her. "Just wait here, I guess."

As we stood there waiting, it got colder. I rubbed my hands together. *I wish I had brought gloves*, I thought.

My skin tingled – and it wasn't just from the cold breeze. I was excited. I was about to get a message – possibly from a ghost! I shivered and realized I was more than a little scared, too.

Jill took a couple of pictures of the mansion. But it was pretty dark outside. So she put her camera away. "It's awfully quiet," she said.

Quiet is right, I thought.

Then it hit me: Nothing was going to happen here. Bethany didn't know what she was talking about. I felt like a complete jerk. I had been fooled. I should never have been taken in by her act.

Suddenly, I heard a noise. It seemed to come from inside the house.

"What was that?" said Phoebe, her voice shaking.

"There it is again!" Ashley whispered.

"Ohhhhh, noooooooo."

It sounded like someone crying . . . or maybe moaning.

"It's just the wind in the trees," Campbell said firmly. I knew she was trying to be sensible.

But it wasn't the wind. I knew it wasn't. My stomach was queasy, and my throat felt tight. Someone – or something – was inside the Stone Ridge Mansion. And whoever – *whatever* – it was had a message for me and my sister.

Bethany had been right!

The moaning got louder. Ashley grabbed my hand.

Then, a kind of ghostly light appeared at a second-floor window. It flickered and jumped. My heart jumped along with it.

And then . . .

"Look!" Ashley breathed, pointing up.

There, in the upstairs window, was the figure of a girl.

But you could see right through her!

Hocus-pocus

She held out her arms and cried: "Mary-Kaaaate!"

I didn't care what Bethany had said.

I didn't care if there was a treasure of gold and jewels waiting for me.

I didn't wait to hear anything else.

I just ran!

Chapter 9

Sunday, Halloween Day

Dear Diary,

When Mary-Kate started to run away from the Stone Ridge Mansion, I raced after her.

Jill, Ginger, Campbell, and Phoebe were right behind me. We all booked as fast as we could.

My heart was pounding in my chest, and I could hardly breathe.

Had we just seen a ghost?

None of us stopped running until we got back to Porter House.

Mary-Kate dashed upstairs to her room. The rest of us followed.

We passed our house mother, Miss Viola, in the hall. She raised a hand. "Mary-Kate . . . girls . . . no running in the – "

But before she could finish, we had all raced into Mary-Kate's room and slammed the door shut behind us.

Mary-Kate flopped on her bed. The rest of us just stood there, breathing hard and looking at one another.

Ginger's freckles stood out against her white face. "I can't b-b-believe it!" she gasped. "It's true. We really saw a – "

Hocus-pocus

"Don't say it," Mary-Kate groaned. "It couldn't be! There's no such things as ghosts!"

"Then why," Campbell asked, catching her breath, "did you run away so fast?"

Mary-Kate was starting to recover. "I was surprised," she said. "That's all."

I turned to Jill. "Did you get any pictures?" I asked.

The rest of the girls turned to her eagerly. But she shook her head. "Sorry," she said. "When I heard the noises, I forgot all about my camera. I was too scared."

There were some Halloween eve parties that night in the dorm, but none of us felt up for it. We stayed together until ten o'clock, when it was lights-out.

By that time, we had all calmed down a bit.

"I guess we'd better get ready for bed," I said. I stood up and headed for the door.

"Thanks for coming with me," Mary-Kate said.

Phoebe and I went back to our rooms and got ready for bed. But believe me, Diary, I didn't sleep very well. I kept dreaming of that white figure, leaning out the window. . . .

So I was pretty tired this morning – Halloween morning, actually.

Even though it was Halloween, I had work to do. Ms. Bloomberg had liked the first draft of my article. Now that I knew about Jill's parents, though, there were a lot of changes I wanted to make.

Phoebe and I met Mary-Kate and Campbell for breakfast in the school dining room.

"How are you doing?" I asked Mary-Kate.

She gave me a shaky smile. "Better," she said. She pointed to the window. It was a bright, sunny day. "It's hard to believe in ghosts on a day like today," she said.

Ginger came up to the table, carrying a tray. She sat down. "There weren't any ghosts," she said firmly. "It must have been our imaginations."

"Ghosts?" Summer squealed, coming up from behind us.

So of course we had to tell her the whole story.

"I'm glad I wasn't there," she said, shaking her head. "I don't know what I would have done!"

"You would have run, just like the rest of us," Jill said, joining us.

We all laughed. That, plus the bright sunshine, made us feel a lot better.

After breakfast, Jill and I headed over to the circus. They would be leaving tomorrow, so this was my last chance to get interviews and for Jill to take pictures.

And Mary-Kate, Jill, and I had a performance that afternoon: We were going to be clowns!

I had to admit. In the daylight, the Stone Ridge Mansion just looked like an old, deserted house. It didn't seem very scary at all.

Of course, I knew better.

When we got to the fair, we checked in with Jill's parents. They told us to come back at about 1:30 to put on our makeup and get ready for the show.

Then Jill and I wandered around, making some last-minute notes and taking pictures.

That's when I noticed my cousin Jeremy. He was talking to Bethany. They were standing near Bethany's trailer, and they didn't see me or Jill.

"Yeah," he was saying. He sounded happy. "I've never seen anything so funny in my entire life! Thanks a lot!"

What was Jeremy talking about? And how did he know Bethany?

I suddenly had a very strange feeling there was something going on here. I tugged Jill's sleeve and pulled her behind Bethany's trailer. "Wait here for a sec," I told her quietly. "I'll be right back. I need to find out something."

Quickly, I sneaked around to Bethany's trailer. Soon, I heard a voice.

It was Bethany's.

"Helping you out was a blast," she was saying. "Anyway, all I had to do was get them there. And I couldn't have done that if you hadn't gotten me all the information about Mary-Kate. That's what made her believe me."

"Yeah." Jeremy laughed. "And the joke is, some of that information came from Ashley!"

My mouth dropped open. I couldn't believe what I was hearing! Jeremy had gotten information from *me* that fooled Mary-Kate? What could it be?

I suddenly remembered something: Jeremy had asked me what to get Mary-Kate for her birthday a few weeks ago.

And I'd told him that she really would love a pair of tickets to some great sports event!

The tickets!

"You should have seen it," Jeremy went on. "The lights and the sound system worked perfectly. And projecting that old movie against the curtain in the window was pure genius. Mary-Kate and Ashley and all their friends ran like scared rabbits!

"Boy, it's lucky I came to the carnival with my roommate a few weeks ago and met you," Jeremy went on. "If I hadn't, I never would have figured out a way to scare them.

"And the best thing of all," he added, "was the pictures I got of Mary-Kate and Ashley screaming and running away. I can't wait to post them on the Harrington Web site."

I gritted my teeth. If Jeremy posted those pictures, we would never hear the end of it.

Bethany said something I couldn't hear.

"You're leaving today? But the circus is in town for a few more days," Jeremy responded. "I'll be back later. Don't go until I get here. I have something really cool for you, just to say thanks."

I was so mad, I almost jumped out of my hiding place to confront Jeremy right there and then.

But I had a better idea.

I snuck back around the trailer. Jill was still standing there, waiting for me.

"Come on," I whispered to her. "We have to find Mary-Kate. There's something we have to do."

Dear Diary,

Oooh, Diary. I am so angry!

That Jeremy is going to be sorry he ever messed with Ashley and me!

Luckily, Ashley had an idea about how to get back at him.

But we needed some help. It had to be from someone he trusted . . . and someone who knew about the circus.

So we went to see Bethany.

We found her packing up her trailer. When she saw us, her eyes narrowed. "What can I do for you girls?" she asked, folding the long paisley scarf that Phoebe had admired.

"That's exactly the question," Ashley said. "What you can do for us."

"We know all about you and Jeremy," I added.

"You do?" Bethany said.

"Is that all you have to say?" Ashley exclaimed.

"Look," Bethany said. "There was no harm in it. He's your cousin. He told me all about you. It was just a practical joke. Besides, this gave me a chance to really study how people react to fortune telling."

"Study?" I was confused.

"I'll tell you the truth," Bethany said. "I'm not really a fortune teller."

"No kidding!" said Ashley.

"Hey," Bethany said. "I fooled your sister, didn't I? I thought I was pretty good at it. Anyway," she went on, "I'm really a freshman at University of New Hampshire, and I'm here doing research for a psychology paper I'm writing. It's on how people can be convinced of almost anything, if they want to be. Even Jeremy doesn't know that.

"Look at it this way, Mary-Kate," Bethany went on. "You got a lot more than you lost. Jeremy actually gave you a stuffed bear and a pair of tickets to a great game. And what did you lose? Not much. Jeremy just got to scare you a little."

"What about the pictures on the Web site?" I demanded.

"It's not that big a deal," Bethany said.

"It is to us!" Ashley said. "Jeremy tricked us. And we're going to get him back."

"And that's where you come in," I added.

"Will you help us?" Ashley said. "I think you owe us one."

Bethany stared at Ashley, and then me. "What do you have in mind?" she asked, a smile slowly spreading across her face.

Chapter 10

Sunday, Halloween Night

Dear Diary,

When word got out that Ashley and I were going to be in the circus, most of the First Form girls decided to come. Even some Second and Third Formers showed up!

A lot of the Harrington boys came, too. Jordan was in the first row, cheering us on. (Jeremy didn't come, of course. Remember, Diary? He doesn't like clowns. But more on that later . . . .)

Anyway, the show went really well. Jill's parents were terrific. They taught us one of their old routines, and we got a lot of laughs.

Plus, we got to drive around in one of those funny little cars. It was awesome.

Jill was great, too. Not only could she make people laugh, but she was especially good with the little kids in the audience.

Of course, she's been practicing most of her life. But I think she has a real talent for it. I could tell her parents were very proud of her.

After the performance, Ashley and I borrowed some of the Jenkinses' clown makeup and a few costumes. We needed them for our plan.

Hocus-pocus

Then Bethany called Jeremy and told him to meet her in the fairgrounds at seven so that he could give her the money he owed her.

It was already getting dark. The grounds were pretty deserted. The rides were almost all packed up, and there were trailers and boxes of stuff everywhere. The circus tent was halfway down. There were mysterious shadows everywhere.

It was a little spooky. Actually, it was a *lot* spooky!

Ashley and I got our makeup on and hid behind Bethany's trailer. She had the window open so we could hear what was going on inside.

At 7:15, Jeremy finally arrived.

"He's always late!" Ashley whispered to me.

Jeremy went into Bethany's trailer.

"Where have you been?" Bethany demanded.

"Sorry," we heard Jeremy say. "Here's the money. Twenty dollars, as promised."

"Thanks," said Bethany. "But I wish you hadn't come so late. It's going to be dark soon. I want to get out of here. This place gives me the creeps."

"How come?" Jeremy asked.

"Haven't you heard?" Bethany told him. "You know. The story about the clowns?"

There was a silence. Then Jeremy asked, "What clowns?"

He sounded nervous. Ashley winked at me. I nodded back at her.

"Oh, yeah," said Bethany, her voice getting lower. "Well, people say that there were some clowns who worked this circus, oh, fifty years ago. They were killed in a freak accident during their last performance. It was on Halloween night. And ever since then . . . "

"Ever since then – what?" Jeremy asked. His voice was a little shaky.

"Well," Bethany went on, "I know it sounds silly. But supposedly, every Halloween, they come back to haunt the circus – the place where they died.

"They try to perform their old act," Bethany added. "And that's one performance I do not want to see."

"Uh . . . yeah," Jeremy said. "Me neither." He cleared his throat. "I'll go with you, okay?"

"Right," Bethany said. "Let's get out of here – now."

That was our cue.

We peeked around the side of the trailer. Bethany was just coming down the little steps. Jeremy was right behind her.

Bethany noticed us out of the corner of her eye and gave us a small wink.

Hocus-pocus

I pressed the button on my MP3 player. Strange-sounding circus music started to play. (I recorded it that morning.)

Ashley began to make groaning noises.

Then we glided out from behind the trailer. And Bethany screamed.

Jeremy took one look at our ghostly white faces and clown costumes and screamed, too. A lot louder than Bethany.

He pushed past Bethany, yelling, and ran down the trailer steps and away.

When he was gone, Jill appeared from behind some boxes. She held up her camera.

"Got them?" I asked.

"You bet," she nodded. "They're going to be great!"

When we got back to Porter House, Jill showed me the pictures on her camera. Then she uploaded them onto her computer.

Jeremy looked really silly with his mouth open, running for his life.

I've got to admit – I couldn't blame him. Ashley and I were pretty scary!

We downloaded the pictures onto my computer. Then we e-mailed Jeremy and attached all of the picture files.

"Jeremy," we wrote. "Nice pictures! We won't show ours if you won't show yours. Deal?"

About ten minutes later, we got an e-mail back.

"Deal," it said simply.

Dear Diary,

Well, I'm happy to report that I don't think Jeremy will be messing with us for a long, long time.

I've never seen anyone look so scared in my entire life!

Jill and I e-mailed our article and the pictures to Ms. B. this afternoon, and she thinks they're terrific.

Almost the whole school came to see Mary-Kate, Jill, and me make clowns of ourselves. It was wonderful.

I'm especially happy for Jill. Her parents are the stars of the school right now, and for the first time in a while she's really proud of them. As a matter of fact, she's thinking about following them into the family business!

Being a clown is the best!

In fact, the only person in town who doesn't think so at the moment is Jeremy. He's still freaked out . . . even though he knows now that *we* were the ones who'd scared him.

Hocus-pocus

So all in all, Diary, this has turned out to be a pretty happy Halloween.

"The only problem is, Jeremy actually did scare us," Mary-Kate admitted to me later that night in my room.

"I know," I told her. "But we got back at him. And besides, she who scares last – "

"Scares best!" we chimed together.

mary-kate olsen   ashley olsen

Holiday Magic

38 Holiday Magic

Dear Diary,

Guess what happened, Diary? Even though my friend, Melina, won our dorm's cook-off, everyone at Porter House wants me to make Chunky Chicken Under Cover after all for our holiday restaurant. So now Melina and I are co-chefs.

But I wish I could be happier. Everyone is counting on me to help win the five-star rating. But I still don't know the secret ingredient that makes Mom's pot pie taste great.

Melina isn't happy, either, Diary. I don't know why. I tried to talk to her.

"Working together will make this project even more fun, Melina," I said. "And a lot less work for you."

Melina just nodded. She looked distracted. Or worried.

Or maybe she just doesn't want to talk, I thought. So I kept talking.

"Because you only have to make *one* dessert, Melina. Not a whole bunch," I said. "Do you need help trying to pick one?"

"No, "Melina snapped. "I can do it."

"I don't mean – " There was no point trying to explain. Melina walked out.

What's her problem, Diary? I know Melina is shy, but she's usually not rude. I thought we were friends. Friends are happy for each other. And they help each other out.

But Melina doesn't want my help.

And she isn't happy that we're both chefs.

Some people want to win no matter what. I just didn't think Melina was like that.

But Melina isn't my only problem. I *still* have to figure out the secret ingredient.

I thought I might recognize the secret ingredient if I saw it. Mrs. Bromsky, the dining hall lady, said I could look at her herbs and spices after dinner Sunday night.

Melina was standing by the big stove when I walked into the dining hall kitchen.

"Hi, Melina!" I was glad to see her. I wanted to fix things between us. "I didn't expect to find you here."

"Mrs. Bromsky gave me permission to cook," Melina said.
She stirred something in a pot on the stove. "She'll be back in a few minutes."

"Mrs. Bromsky gave me permission to check the spices," I said. I took a step toward the stove. "What are you making?"

Melina moved so I couldn't look into the pot. "It's just an experiment."

I suspected Melina was guarding a secret recipe. Recipes are a chef's most prized possessions. If Melina didn't want to discuss her recipe, that was okay with me. I changed the subject.

"Maybe you can help me," I said.

Melina was the *perfect* person to ask about the secret ingredient. She had probably learned a lot from her famous chef mother.

"Help with what?" Melina asked.

"One of the seasonings on my mom's recipe is too faded to read," I explained. Everything about the pot pie I baked for the cook-off was the same as my mom's. Except for the taste.

I moved to the racks of spices on the counter. Mrs. Bromsky arranged them in alphabetical order. I read the labels on the jars to myself.

All spice, basil, bay leaves. . .

"The missing seasoning gives the sauce a zesty tang," I told Melina. "Do you have any idea what spice it might be?"

I read more labels to myself. *Celery salt, chives, cinnamon, cloves* . . .

"Different blends of herbs and spices create different aromas and flavors," Melina said.

"Right," I agreed. "That's why I need to know what seasoning I'm missing."

"But there are a zillion possible combinations," Melina said. "So I can't possibly guess."

"Oh." I nodded. "I see your point. Thanks anyway."

Melina's explanation made sense. But I couldn't give up. My mom's pot pie would be a total flop without the secret ingredient.

I kept reading. *Dill, garlic salt, ginger* . . .

"Oh, no!" Melina shrieked and jumped back from the stove.

"What's the matter?" I sprang to help her.

"See what you made me do!" Melina glared at me.

I looked at the pot on the stove. Melina's mysterious mixture was boiling over. Dark brown goo bubbled inside the pot. Globs dribbled down the sides.

"Me?" I was stunned.

"I stopped stirring to talk to you," Melina said. "This is ruined!"

I didn't want to say anything, but I think Melina's recipe was ruined *before* it boiled over. Whatever it was, it smelled awful!

And Melina saw me wrinkle my nose.

"Are you making fun of me, Ashley?" Melina's eyes flashed. She was furious.

"No, Melina!" I couldn't let her think that! "Honest."

"Now I have to clean up this mess." Melina turned the stove off.

"I'm really sorry," I said. "Let me help you – "

"No thanks, Ashley." Melina moved the pan to a cold burner. "I just wanted to be left alone."

I didn't want to make things worse. I left, but I was upset, too.

Melina and I were becoming good friends before the cook-off. Now it looks like our friendship is over because of a silly contest.

Dear Diary,

I helped Rhonda load the rolls into her car. Then I went back to Burger Bistro with her. I sure didn't expect to find Dana Woletsky waiting for us!

"What are you doing here, Dana?" I asked.

"I'm writing a story about the Holiday Dinner for the school newspaper," Dana explained. "Doing something nice for police officers and fire-fighters is a great seasonal topic."

"And we appreciate the publicity, Dana," Rhonda said.

Dana looked at Rhonda. "What's Mary-Kate doing here?"

"She's helping me with the Holiday Dinner," Rhonda said. "It's too bad I can't get more student volunteers. I'm short of help because so many families want to come."

"Just like us," Mary-Kate said. "Porter House has so many reservations some people might have to eat standing up!"

"Our dorm has lots of people coming, too," Dana said. Dana always has to act as if she's better than I am.

"I'm glad we're all doing so well," Rhonda said.

I realized Rhonda didn't want us to argue. Dana took the hint and stopped bickering, too.

"The Holiday Dinner is very important to me," Rhonda went on. "It's a lucky thing Mary-Kate already knows how things work at the Burger Bistro. At least I can count on her. I could use ten more like you, Mary-Kate." Rhonda smiled. "I have to check the phone messages. Be right back."

Dana didn't say anything until Rhonda closed the office door. "So you're waiting on tables at Rhonda's Holiday Dinner? How does everyone at Porter House feel about that?"

"They know I can handle both jobs, Dana," I said. "It's no big deal."

Dana arched an eyebrow. "Gee, I think someone who can be in two places at once is a very big deal."

Huh? I blinked.

"What do you mean?" I asked.

"The Holiday Dinner is *Saturday*." Dana couldn't hide her glee. "The same night the First Form restaurants are open for the White Oak Winter Festival."

I never thought to check the date, Diary! And every time Rhonda and I started talking about the details, something cut the conversation short.

This is a *huge* problem.

I can't back out on Rhonda now. She doesn't have enough help, and I promised.

But I can't let Ashley and everyone else at Porter House down, either.

And I definitely can't be in two places at once.

What am I going to do?

mary-kateandashley

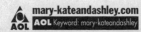

mary-kateandashley

Sweet 16

(1) *Never Been Kissed*   (0 00 714879 8)
(2) *Wishes and Dreams*   (0 00 714880 1)
(3) *The Perfect Summer*   (0 00 714881 X)

HarperCollins*Entertainment*

PARACHUTE PRESS

DUALSTAR PUBLICATIONS

mary-kateandashley.com
AOL Keyword: mary-kateandashley

mary-kateandashley

TWO of a kind ™

HarperCollins*Entertainment*

PARACHUTE PRESS

DUALSTAR PUBLICATIONS

mary-kateandashley.com
AOL Keyword: mary-kateandashley

mary-kateandashley
TWO of a kind ™

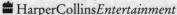

HarperCollins*Entertainment*

 PARACHUTE PRESS

 DUALSTAR PUBLICATIONS

 mary-kateandashley.com
AOL Keyword: mary-kateandashley

TM & © 2002 Dualstar Entertainment Group, LLC.

mary-kateandashley
Be a part of Mary-Kate and Ashley's world on www.mary-kateandashley.com!
LOG ON!
www.mary-kateandashley.com brings you all the latest news and views, sizzling style tips and hot Hollywood happenings!
Exclusive access behind-the-scenes of Mary-Kate and Ashley's movies!
Real Talk for Real Girls
Each week read fresh features on fashion, friends and feeling your very best!
www.mary-kateandashley.com! Real Talk for Real Girls!
DUALSTAR ONLINE
mary-kateandashley.com
AOL Keyword: mary-kateandashley
TM & © 2004 Dualstar Entertainment Group, LLC. All Rights Reserved.

MARY-KATE OLSEN ASHLEY OLSEN

BIG FUN IN THE BIG APPLE!

MARY-KATE OLSEN AND
ASHLEY OLSEN IN THE
BIG SCREEN HIT

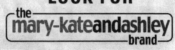